By Daniel Postgate

For Rochelle

SMELLY BILL'S WHIFFY WEEKEND

By Daniel Postgate

meadowside
CHILDREN'S BOOKS

Contents

Meet the Family...

Prologue

THE LAST SAUSAGE

"Look at this!" exclaimed Dad, holding up one foot with a slipper on it.

The end of the slipper had been gnawed away and Dad's toes were sticking out.

"It's too much!" he moaned.

"And he's been at the butter," said Mum. "Someone left it out on the kitchen table and there's a big bite out of it."

The children were also far from happy. Jasmine's favourite doll was now headless and Angus's football, once hard and round, was now squidgy and flat ... with tooth-marks in it.

"That dog is driving us all absolutely crazy," sighed Mum.

"I think we all deserve a break," said Dad. "Let's pack the tent in the car and go for a quiet weekend away." He thrust his hand into the air. "Who's with me?" he cried.

The others eagerly raised their hands too.

"Let's do it!" Mum declared.

"But what about Bill?" asked Jasmine.

Dad beckoned the others to come close. "Sunny Meadow Kennels," he hissed.

Bill the dog was on his back, in his basket, in the kitchen. He had been asleep, but the words 'Sunny Meadow Kennels' had woken him with a start.

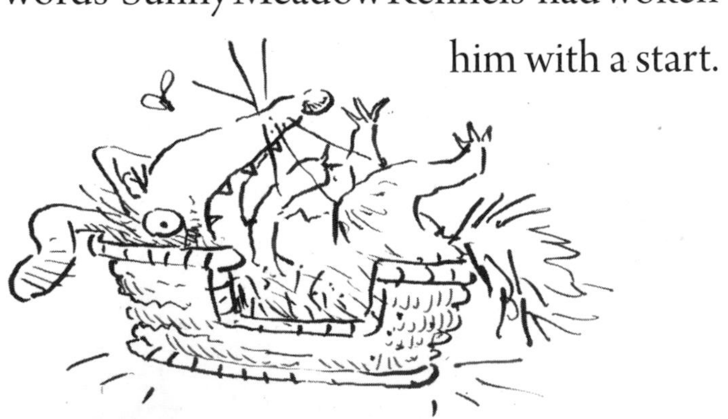

If there was one place he hated, it was Sunny Meadow Kennels.

The family heard the dog-flap go flip-flap.

"I think he heard you," said Jasmine.

"Never mind, let's get everything packed-up and ready to go," said Dad. "We'll deal with Bill later." He narrowed his eyes and tapped his nose. "I have a plan."

Once everything was packed and ready, Dad gathered everyone around and whispered his plan.

Shortly afterwards Angus went into the garden. Bill was on the roof of the garden shed, watching Angus's every move.

"Oh look," said Angus in a loud voice, "I've got some fresh plump sausages!"

Bill's ears raised slightly.

"I'll just take them out of the packet," said Angus. "Oops, I've dropped one. Oh no, I've dropped another. And another ..."

Angus dropped the sausages in a trail leading to the back door, then he went inside.

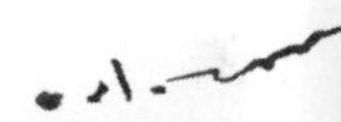

He laid the last sausage on the mat just inside the door, centimetres from the dog-flap.

"Well done," said Dad, grasping a large rubble sack. "Now we just have to wait."

They didn't have to wait long.

Mum peeked out of the kitchen window, then ducked down.

"He's taking the bait," she mouthed, and gave Dad the 'thumbs-up'.

"Excellent," whispered Dad, "Jasmine, you know what to do."

Outside, Bill cautiously made his way down from the roof of the shed. He briefly sniffed at the first sausage he came to, carefully looked around, then turned his attention back to the sausage and gobbled it up. Quickly, he moved onto the next, then the next. With each sausage he moved ever closer to the back door. Eventually, when every sausage in the garden had been devoured, he pushed his snout through the dog-flap and sniffed deeply.

Inside, the family held their breath; not daring to move or make a noise.

The last sausage was just out of Bill's

reach. He had a choice – he could be happy with the sausages he had already eaten and leave the last one; or take a risk and plunge through the flap, get the sausage and be back out before the enemy had time to strike.

It wasn't much of a choice really. Bill knew that there was no way in the world he could leave that last sausage.

In a flash he dived in through the flap, snatched the sausage and was back out before Dad had a chance to pounce.

However, the family had been far more cunning than Bill had expected ...

Jasmine, with another sack, had come in through the back gate and had snuck up the garden path.

So when Bill came back out the flap with the last sausage in his teeth, he charged straight into Jasmine's waiting sack, and was caught.

The family all congratulated each other on a brilliant piece of teamwork.

Sunny Meadow Kennels wasn't sunny, nor was it a meadow. In fact it was a concrete prison for dogs.

The last time Bill was there he had

escaped. Miss Grinder, the owner of the kennels, had chased after him. She didn't catch him, but she did fall in a ditch and she did get stung by a bee. So Bill was no way her favourite dog.

"Ah, Bill. So we meet again," said Miss Grinder, with a scowl.

"He won't be any trouble," said Dad hopefully, as he handed over the lead with an unhappy Bill on the end.

Miss Grinder's face then broke into a frightening grin. "Oh no," she said brightly, "I'll make sure of that. You have a nice holiday Mr Cooper, and leave the dog to me."

"Erm – okay," said Dad. "Thanks."

Dad watched as Bill was led away, down the concrete alleyway with cages of barking dogs on either side. For a moment he felt rather sad to see Bill go. He turned to see the family in the car, they looked sad too. No matter how naughty Bill was, they still loved him.

"Be nice to him!" Dad called after Miss Grinder, then trudged back to the car.

"Be nice to him," repeated Miss Grinder in a mocking voice. She pulled hard on Bill's lead. "Stop struggling you brute," she hissed.

"I haven't forgotten the last time you were here. The mayhem you caused, the misery you put me through. I have a special cell for you, where you can howl as much as you like but no one will hear your cries." Then she laughed in a very nasty way.

She led Bill past all the other cages until she reached a thick steel door. As she pulled the door open Bill saw with horror the windowless room inside.

"In you go!" she clucked.

Bill scrambled backwards, desperate to get away.

"Putting up a fight, eh?" she sneered. "Well, you've picked the wrong lady, buster!"

She pulled and pulled at Bill's lead until 'SNAP!' The lead broke and Miss Grinder tumbled backwards into the darkened room.

Bill couldn't believe his luck! He ran at the door and pushed at it with all his might. Miss Grinder's shrill cry was cut short as the door slammed shut and the lock clicked.

Bill dashed down the concrete alleyway. The dogs howled in their cages, cheering him on. At the end of the alleyway he saw a lever on the wall. He jumped up and grabbed it with his teeth, pulling it down. The doors on all the cages suddenly clicked open, and dogs of every kind – big dogs; small dogs; thin dogs; fat dogs – sprang free, barking joyfully with their new-found freedom.

Bill could see his family's car making its

way down the gravel path. He had to be quick, otherwise they'd get away.

"Do you think he'll be okay?" asked Jasmine inside the car.

"Oh yes," said Mum.

"Miss Grinder is a lovely lady," said Dad. "She'll take very good care of him." Then he smiled and let out a sigh of relief. "And just think, a whole weekend without Bill. Oh joy of joys!"

The car pulled out of the gravel path and roared off down the road, with a happy family inside... and a dog on the roof.

PART 1:

CAMPSITE CHAOS

RHINOCEROS AND CHIPS

It was already starting to get dark when the family arrived at the campsite.

They unpacked the tent and then went about putting it up, too busy to notice Bill skulking off along the hedge behind them. Bill found a gap in the hedge. He struggled through it into the open countryside beyond and went off to explore.

Once the tent was up, Dad got the cooking stuff ready and Mum sorted out the inside of the tent while the children went off to have a look around.

"Was that your dog I saw creeping

around?!" someone shouted.

Dad looked up from fiddling with a gas canister and saw a man sitting with his wife outside a nearby tent. The man had a huge bushy moustache and his wife was reading a newspaper.

"No, no. Our dog's back home in the kennels," said Dad with a friendly smile.

"Glad to hear it," shouted the man. "Can't stand dogs! All that barking and running

about, it drives me up the wall! Although I have to say I do like eating them!"

"I beg your pardon?" said Dad in surprise.

"Dog meat – very tasty! In some countries they eat dogs you know! I've tried it, it's very nice! I've eaten quite a few unusual animals as it happens. Have you ever tried badger meat?!"

Dad shook his head. "I'm a vegetarian actually," he said.

The man ignored Dad and carried on shouting about eating animals. "Badgers are alright but here's a tip: you have to cook them slowly, otherwise they're a bit tough! But eating isn't the best thing! Do you want to know what the best thing is?!"

"Being sick afterwards?" suggested Dad.

"No! It's the hunt! Stalking the creature! The battle of Man against Beast! Over

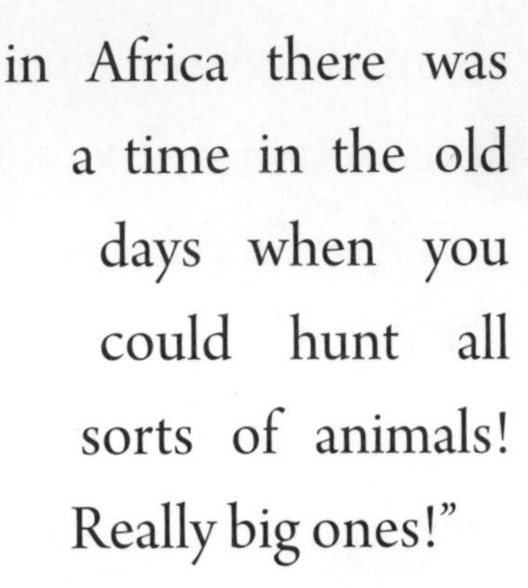

in Africa there was a time in the old days when you could hunt all sorts of animals! Really big ones!"

The man held up one hand and put the other to his cheek, as if he was holding an invisible gun. "My father told me about his adventures in Africa!"

"Your father's never left Wigan," interrupted his wife.

"Please Valerie, don't interrupt," shouted the man. "My father shot elephants, rhinoceroses, hippopotami; oh all sorts!"

"And then he ate them?" Dad asked.

The man made a banging sound with his mouth, as if shooting invisible bullets

from his invisible gun, then he thought about Dad's question. "I don't think so!" he finally shouted. "He had quite an appetite but he probably couldn't manage a whole elephant! He might have had a bit of one!"

"Perhaps he had a bit of elephant and kept the rest for sandwiches for the next day," suggested Dad.

"Perhaps!" shouted the man. "Anyway, the point is shooting animals makes you into a man! A real man! When you've got a twenty-tonne polar bear charging at you it's not the time to get all wimpy and weedy – you must be brave!"

"I didn't think you got polar bears in Africa," said Dad helpfully.

The man ignored Dad and carried on shouting.

"The trouble these days is you can't shoot anything without everyone making a dreadful fuss! Take that dog I saw earlier. Ideally I should be able to track it down and blam!! Roast dog all round! Everyone goes to bed with a full tummy! What's wrong with that?!"

"What's wrong with that?!" cried Dad. "Everything – it's cruel and … and nasty."

"But natural," shouted the man. "Creatures eat each other every day of the week. The world is like an enormous restaurant!"

"Anyway, could you stop shouting about eating animals?" asked Dad. "It's making me feel a bit ill. Perhaps you could shout about something else instead?"

The man thought about this, but decided there wasn't anything else he was interested in shouting about. "Nice

chatting to you. I better start making the dinner now!" he shouted.

When the man got up from his deck chair Dad noticed how extraordinarily big and baggy his shorts were.

"What are you having for dinner?" Dad asked. "Baby elephant burger? Rhinoceros and chips?"

"Sadly not!" shouted the man, climbing into his tent. "Just fish finger sandwiches!"

His wife looked over her newspaper at Dad. "He likes them with the crusts cut off," she said with a grin.

"What a terrible person," whispered Mum peeping out from their tent. "Did you hear what he said about eating dogs? Thank goodness Bill's not here."

COUNTRY PANCAKE

But of course Bill was there, and he was having a marvellous time.

He'd never been to the countryside before. He'd been to the park, but the park was nothing like this. All sorts of exciting smells filled his nostrils, sending him snuffling across the fields.

In one field Bill found some large, strange looking beasts lazily chewing on their cud. He'd never seen cows before. He barked at them for a while and they looked at him with their big brown eyes, then ignored him. One of the cows raised her tail and

dropped a pile of dung onto the field. Bill was fascinated. He immediately went over to investigate. The dung had settled into a steaming brown pool. Bill sniffed at it. It didn't smell of anything very much, but there was a lot of it. Then he flipped himself over and landed with a splat right on top of it. He wriggled and writhed on the gloriously sludgy mess until his fur was well and truly coated.

Bill found that there were lots more of these cow-cakes around the field. Some were quite fresh while others were old with

a hard, crusty skin. When he rolled in these ones he found the crust, once broken, gave way to the sweet treasure beneath; sloppy and nicely warm from a day in the sun. The older cakes had a far richer stink to them too and Bill was sure if he could find some fox droppings to go with his fine new coat of dung he would have a medley of smells which would be something truly fantastic, better than anything he had ever made back home.

Just then Bill spotted a fox on the other side of the field, swooping through the long undergrowth. Barking, he ran over, hoping to make friends. The fox stopped, pricked up its ears and stared at Bill for a moment, then quickly dashed off into some bramble bushes.

Bill followed.

It wasn't long before Bill was completely lost in a dark world of spiky brambles, twigs and scratchy plants. And he hated it. To make matters worse, there were horrible flying things – gnats and midges and mosquitoes that come out when the sun goes down. They nibbled at him and got in his eyes and ears.

Bill now thought that the countryside wasn't such a wonderful place after all, and he was also beginning to feel rather hungry.

He decided to get back to the campsite as soon as possible.

After a great deal of whimpering and scrambling and growling, Bill struggled out of the bushes and tumbled back out into the field. The cow mess he'd caked himself in had acted like a kind of glue, sticking bits of bramble and plant and branch to his fur. He no longer looked like Bill at all, in fact he didn't even look like a dog … or anything else on this Earth.

It was dark when he finally scrambled through the hedge back into the campsite.

He heard voices near the family tent. A man nearby was shouting over at the family.

"Do you know what I'd really like to shoot?!" bellowed the man. He didn't wait for a reply. "A yeti. Yes, the great beast who lives in the icy wastelands of the Himalayas. Imagine that, eh?! Coming face to face with such a giant, hairy creature. Not a moment for wimpy weeds I can tell you! I wouldn't be scared though, oh no not me!"

"Oh, is that the time?" someone shouted back. It was Dad. "Must go to bed now… good night, sweet dreams."

"I wonder what yeti-meat tastes like?!" shouted the man.

"That's enough now, Frank," said his wife. "I think everyone's heard quite enough about shooting and eating things."

Bill watched as everyone went into their tents. He decided to lay low and wait until the whole campsite was quiet, then he'd

go on a forage for food. There were bound to be some nice pickings left outside the tents.

He watched as campers went off to a small concrete shed with their small bags and towels, then returned to their tents. One by one, little lights and torches went off until the whole campsite was silent and dark.

CHILLI SAUCE

When he was sure everyone was safely tucked up in their tents, Bill made his way from one tent to the next, snuffling around the guy-ropes in search of goodies.

He found two half-chewed spare-ribs left on a paper plate and happily crunched on them. Some black things, discarded by a smouldering barbecue were also discovered and quickly snaffled up. He also found a saucepan full of barbecue favoured baked beans – very nice. Outside another tent was a pot of thick, dark-red goo with the lid left off. The label on the pot said: Chilli sauce. Caution: Very hot!

But it was too dark to read it, and Bill was a dog,. so he couldn't read it anyway. Within a moment he'd eaten the lot and was busy licking the bottom of the pot when the heat from the chilli sauce suddenly turned his mouth into a furnace! Whimpering and running around the campsite, he desperately searched for some water. He remembered the concrete shed where

people went to wash and ran over to it with his mouth open and his tongue flapping to keep cool.

He ran into the shed and was relieved to find a toilet there. Clambering up onto the toilet bowl, he thrust his muzzle into the murky water and drank deeply. He drank and drank until the fire in his mouth finally eased to a warm tingle.

Then he heard a noise on the metal roof of the shed. A pitter-patter at first, which quickly built up to a roar. It was pouring with rain outside.

Bill crept out of the shed, cautiously looking up at the sky. He hated rain almost as much as he hated baths. He had

to get back to the family tent as quickly as possible.

It was really pelting down when he got to the tents. In the chaos of the rain, he couldn't remember which tent was which, and which tent belonged to the family. He had to just choose one, any one. Picking one out, he nuzzled his way past the zipper and struggled inside.

"What was that?" said a man's voice.

"Nothing dear, go back to sleep," said a woman's voice.

The voices didn't belong to Mum and Dad, that much Bill knew, but he decided to stay where he was rather than go back out in the rain. He would keep very quiet and still, and hopefully the people would go back to sleep.

Unfortunately the mixture of baked

beans and chilli sauce began to have a strange and not very nice effect on Bill's tummy. He could feel it growling and bubbling.

Suddenly his tummy let out a sound like a lion roaring underwater.

"Did you hear that?!" exclaimed the man's voice.

"Just a bit of thunder, Frank. Go back to sleep," mumbled the woman's voice.

Now Bill could feel his tummy bloating up like a balloon.

Then … 'PFFFFFFF'.

Luckily, the sound wasn't loud and rasping. But oh, the smell!

"Good grief!" yelled the old man's voice. "What a terrible pong! Valerie, was that you?!"

"No it certainly was not!" exclaimed the woman's voice. "Pooh! Goodness me! It must have been you Frank! You know what they say – whoever smelt it, dealt it!"

"It wasn't me!" declared the man. "I think I'd know if I'd blown off!"

"Well if it wasn't you, and it wasn't me ... then WHO?"

There was a click and the glare of a torch flashed around the inside of the tent. Bill caught sight of the man with the big bushy moustache just at the same time the man caught sight of him.

No one could have slept through the horrendous scream that went up from the man's tent and echoed around the campsite. People stuck their heads out of their tents to see what was going on. The man had run out into the rain and was slipping around on the soggy grass in nothing but his pyjamas, howling and gasping for breath.

At the family's tent, the zip suddenly zuzzed open. Mum quickly grabbed her torch and shone it at the terrified man who had shoved his face, shiny and red with a soggy moustache, into their tent.

"Save yourselves!" he spluttered.

"What's the matter?" Mum yelled.

"A creature! A monster! Like nothing I've ever seen! It was in my tent! Now it's roaming around! No one is safe!

It'll eat us all!" the man screamed. Then he was gone.

Mum gathered the children together as they listened to the man running from tent to tent crying out his warning. He had found two metal pots and was banging them together to make his cries all the more urgent.

Angus peeped out of the tent and watched the mayhem outside. Dozens of torches flashed this way and that as frightened

campers, still in their nighties and pyjamas, ran this way and that through the pelting rain. He heard car engines turning over and roaring into life, families barking orders at each other. He saw headlights come on as cars and caravans skidded off across the field.

Then, as quickly as it had begun, the chaos was over. The campsite was silent and dark once again. Even the rain had stopped.

"Everyone's gone," said Angus, looking back at the family.

"Do you think we should go too?" Mum asked her husband urgently.

Dad was deep inside his sleeping bag. Mum prodded him with her foot.

"Do you think we should go?" she repeated.

Dad's head slowly appeared from out the top of his bag.

"I – I don't know," Dad said in a trembling voice. "Jasmine, have a look out of the tent, see if you can see anything dangerous."

"You look out of the tent!" said Jasmine. "You're Dad after all. Come on, be brave."

Reluctantly, Dad clambered from the safety of his bag. The family waited patiently while he slipped his feet into his slippers. Eventually, he was ready. Mum handed him a torch. "Good luck," she said,

and patted him on the back.

Dad slowly stepped from the tent and flashed the torch around. "Is there anybody there?" he whispered.

There was a whimpering noise.

"Did you hear that?" said Mum.

"What?" said Dad.

"A whimpering noise," said Mum.

"Yes," said Dad. "It was me."

There was a snuffling noise.

"What about the snuffling noise?" asked Angus.

"That wasn't me," said Dad. The torch light caught the glow of two eyes just a few metres away.

"AAAAAAAARGH!" exclaimed Dad, dropping the torch. He flung himself back into the tent. "It's coming for us!" he wailed.

The family backed into the furthest corner of the tent and hugged each other in terror.

At the slit of the tent entrance a nose appeared, then a snout with whiskers, then two beady eyes.

"AAAAAAAARGH," the family cried together.

"Hold on," said Angus. "Isn't that … isn't that … Bill?!"

BILL THE HERO

Bill wagged his tail and grinned at the family. The downpour of rain had washed the worst of the cow dung and bits of bramble from his fur and he looked like a dog again.

"Good heavens above, you're right," gasped Mum, "it is Bill."

"Bill!" shouted Dad. "You nearly scared us all half to death!"

"But – but how did he get here?" asked Angus, shaking his head in disbelief.

"I know! It's just like a film I saw on the telly," said Jasmine excitedly. "It was called

'Lassie Come Home'. Lassie was a dog who travelled a great distance, had fantastic adventures and went through terrible danger. Just so he could be with the people she loved! And that's exactly what Bill has done!"

"And," said Angus, "he arrived just in time to see off that monster that was roaming around outside. Bill has probably saved our lives! He's a hero!"

Mum and the children all gathered round Bill. They didn't touch him because he was still pretty filthy, but they grinned at him and said nice things.

"Hold on, hold on," said Dad. "Jasmine, I like your theory on how Bill got here but there's one problem."

"What's that?" asked Jasmine.

"It's total rubbish," explained Dad. "There is no way on Earth he could have got here in just a few hours, it would have taken him days, if not weeks. And how would he know where we are? Even I didn't know which campsite we'd stop at."

"It's a miracle," cooed Mum. "There are some things in life that can never be explained... What adventures Bill must have had. If only he could talk."

"And as for Bill scaring away some monstrous beast," said Dad. "Come on, Bill's even scared of next door's cat!"

The family ignored Dad and carried on fussing over their hero. Mum got a towel and gave him a rubdown. Angus found some biscuits and fed them to him. Even

Dad eventually forgot his doubts about how Bill had got there. He gave Bill a pat on the head and told him he was a good old boy. Then he scrunched up the picnic blanket so Bill had a nice soft nest to sleep in. Eventually, they all got back into their sleeping bags, switched off their camping lamp, and settled down to sleep.

Only a few moments later... 'PFFFFFF!'

Dad opened one eye. His nose twitched. Then he sat up.

"Euuurgh!" he exclaimed. "What an unholy stink! Bill, if you do that again you can get out of the tent!"

"Dad, don't be so cruel," said Jasmine. "Remember, he's our hero. Without him,

we might have been eaten by that enormous horrible monster."

"Yes, I suppose you're right," said Dad.

Then Bill let out another stinker.

"Right, that's it!" said Dad, kicking his way out of his sleeping bag. "I'm sleeping in the car."

Bill's constant blowing off eventually proved too much for the rest of the family, and one by one they all left the tent and joined Dad in the car.

By the time the sun had appeared behind the trees to begin its daily trip across the sky, the Cooper family were all packed in their car, desperately trying to get comfortable. Meanwhile Bill languished in the tent, dreaming about chasing rabbits ... and farting.

PART II:
SEASIDE SHENANIGANS

Beside the Seaside

Stretching and yawning the next morning, the Cooper family finally emerged from their car to start a new day.

They looked around at the sorry scene of the campsite with its deserted tents, and soggy grass with skid-marks where the cars and caravans had left in such a hurry the night before. The family decided it was time that they left too. They quickly dressed, packed the tent up, shoved it into the boot of the car and roared away.

They were heading for the seaside, another place Bill had never been before.

After a short drive, they went over the brow of a hill and saw a vast expanse of shimmering sea before them.

"Look!" yelled Angus and Jasmine excitedly, and Bill let out a couple of happy barks.

"Oh I do like to be beside the seaside, oh I do like to be beside the sea ..." sang Mum and Dad as they trundled down the hill and into the seaside town of Frosbie-on-Sea. They were quite early so they were able to find a parking place right by the sea front.

Then they saw a sign which said: NO DOGS ON BEACH.

"Oh for goodness sake," exclaimed Angus. "Why can't dogs go on the beach? I mean, what trouble could Bill possibly cause?"

"Hmm. Well, that's a shame," said Dad looking at the sign. "Sorry Bill, rules is rules. You're going to have to stay in the car."

Bill sat with his snout pressed against the glass of the car window as he watched the family go off to have their fun.

"We won't be too long!" Dad shouted back at him, and he gave him a sad little wave.

Bill sat and waited, he waited and waited. At least five minutes passed. He was starting to feel very bored. He watched as more and more happy sun-seekers arrived with their deck chairs and buckets and spades, and brightly coloured beach-balls; all looking forward to a fun day on the golden sands. With each joyous arrival Bill felt a little more sad and little more left out.

The car window had been left slightly open so Bill would have fresh air. He pushed his snout into the gap and wiggled it about. Gradually, inch by inch, he managed to push the window down and down until the

gap was finally deep enough for a dog to squeeze through it. And that's exactly what Bill did. He squeezed through the gap in the window and tumbled to freedom.

Hey-presto!

The second magnificent escape of the weekend was complete!

CANDYFLOSS MONSTER

The sign, NO DOGS ON BEACH meant nothing to Bill of course. He marched straight past it and padded off across the sand, which was heating up nicely under the morning sun. Wisely, he chose to head away from the family. Knowing that if they spotted him they'd put him back in the car, or at least try to, and he didn't fancy that.

Bill splashed about in the sea and chased after some seagulls; he thought the seaside was a wonderful place!

Soon, he came upon a very strange sight: a stripy little tent stood in the middle of

the beach. In a square hole at the top of the tent, two small people were arguing. One was a woman, holding a baby. The other was an ugly looking man cuddling a large club. The man was using the club to hit the woman with, and at the same time he was shouting, 'That's the way to do it!' in a horribly shrill voice. What made the scene even more horrifying to Bill was that a gang of young children were sitting in front of the tent, watching this ghastly event … and laughing!

Of course the children were simply enjoying a Punch and Judy puppet show. But Bill didn't know this, he was just a dog and knew nothing of puppet shows. What he saw was a man being very, very cruel to a defenceless woman with a baby. He was appalled. The hair on the back of his neck

stood up, he scowled and showed his teeth, then let out a deep, throaty growl.

Barking and snarling, Bill charged past the children and scrambled under the tent. In the darkness inside, Bill sank his teeth into something, which felt very much like a leg. In fact, it was a leg.

"AAAAAARGH!" came a cry from just above him.

Bill held on tight as the leg swung and

shook. Suddenly, the man to whom the leg belonged keeled over sideways. With the split and splinter of thin wood snapping he brought the tent down with him. Both Bill and the man found themselves helplessly wrapped up in the cloth of the tent.

"Get off!" shouted the man, kicking Bill away. Bill let go and struggled to free himself from the mangle of cloth. When he did finally emerge, he found himself nose to nose with an extremely angry looking man.

"What are you doing!" yelled the man, sitting up and shaking his fists at Bill. His fists still had the Punch and Judy puppets on them. So the man looked like he was shaking two very small people.

Confused, Bill decided the best thing to do was to leave right away.

All the children thought what had happened was part of the show. And they loved it! They laughed and clapped, and yelled for more.

"Come back!" they shouted as Bill galloped off along the beach, closely followed by the man waving his hands and shouting some very rude words.

Bill could still hear the man behind him as he weaved his way through the maze of sunbathers. He had to find somewhere to hide, and quick.

He spotted a brightly coloured van with signs and rubber rings hanging from it. It also had a hatchway. He decided the best thing to do was to jump through the hatchway, which is exactly what he did.

Inside, he fell straight into a spinning tub. And for about a minute he rolled around not knowing where he was or which way was up. He had unexpectedly landed in a candyfloss machine.

"Get out! GET OUT!" shouted the woman in the van. She flung her hands about knocking a pot of hundreds and thousands over Bill, who already had a thick coat of candyfloss over him. When he did finally manage to scramble free of

the spinning machine and jump back out of the hatchway, he looked like a bright pink cloud on legs, speckled with hundreds and thousands. He stumbled about on the sand, trying to stop his head from spinning. Then started running again.

"Hey, come back here!" shouted the woman from the van. But Bill had no intention of coming back anywhere. He raced straight past a very surprised looking Punch and Judy man and back past the gang of children who squealed with delight at the sight of the candyfloss creature. One little girl managed to grab a clump of floss off Bill as he went by, and chomped on it greedily. The other children felt left out and decided they wanted a bit of the candyfloss creature too. So they all set off after him.

Bill sprinted along the beach with a gaggle of kids not far behind, and not far behind them was the Punch and Judy man,

and not far behind him was the candyfloss woman. Bill wasn't sure the seaside was such a wonderful place after all.

BANANA DRAMA

Just ahead of him, Bill saw another very strange sight: a large inflatable banana with three people sitting on it. It was slipping down the beach and into the sea. Bill decided he had no choice but to take his chances on the Banana. He jumped on board just as the Banana hit the sea and quickly picked up speed. The banana was being pulled by a speedboat, which was now roaring through the waves. Bill hung on as best he could and glanced back at the rapidly disappearing beach where a crowd of people, all eager to get their hands on

him, stood waving and shouting.

It had been a very close escape, but Bill had the feeling that he was now in more danger than ever before – zooming off through the sea on a giant banana wasn't his idea of being safe and sound.

He tried to communicate with his three fellow travellers, by barking at them as loudly as he could. All three turned around, looked shocked, lost their balance, screamed, and fell into the sea. Bill looked back and saw them bobbing about in their life jackets. Soon they were just dots in the distance. Bill struggled along the shaft

of the banana as it swooped and banged through the waves. He howled and barked to try and get the speedboat driver's attention, but it was no good – nothing could be heard over the roar of the engine. Eventually Bill reached the banana's tip; it was tied to the boat by a rope. Bill lunged at the rope in a desperate attempt to bite through it. But he missed, and instead he sank his teeth into the yellow plastic.

There was a tearing noise and the banana let out a loud roar as the air inside it flew out, and it shot off, along with Bill, in the opposite direction to the boat. It skimmed

across the waves at a tremendous speed, at one point actually taking to the air, before it eventually fell into the sea; all floppy and flaccid.

For a moment Bill sank deep down into the silent darkness of water. His skinny legs started pumping as hard as they could and he managed to come gargling and gasping to the surface. Time and again he went under, and time and again he struggled to the surface. The waves crashed against him as he felt his strength ebbing away.

Just as he felt he could fight the sea no longer he found himself tangled up in something solid. Suddenly, he was pulled upwards. Now he was helplessly dangling in a net, and a moment later he found himself flopping onto the deck of a boat, surrounded by a hundred flickering fish.

A large lady with a happy red face stared down at him. "Well I'll be a lobster's Auntie, you're a funny looking fish," she cried. "Susan, come and look at this!"

Another lady appeared from the cabin and stood with her hands on her hips, grinning at the sight of Bill tangled up in the net.

"You know what that is," she said. "That's a dog fish." And the ladies both had a jolly good laugh.

The lady with the happy red face untangled a soggy Bill from the net and gave him a really good rubdown with a towel until he was nice and fluffy and dry. Then she went to help her friend with the rest of their catch; picking up the glistening fish and tossing them into a large crate.

After a meal of fresh sardines and a bowl of strong, sugary tea, Bill felt like his old self again. Refreshed, he went to the front of the boat and held his snout high, enjoying the cool, salty breeze. He listened to the cry of the hungry seagulls and the chug-chug-chug of the boat as it bobbed up and down and rode the waves, back towards the shore.

One of the ladies busied herself with sorting through the fish while the other steered the boat from the cabin. And they both sang sweetly about their life on the open waves:

"Some girls like to bathe in milk,
And drive around in cars.
Some girls like to dress in silk,
And dance beneath the stars.
Some girls wears the finest pearls,
And eat the finest dishes.
But we're not like those kind of girls…
We like to catch big fishes."

The boat eventually chugged into Frosbie-on-Sea's harbour and one of the ladies hopped onto the quayside with a thick rope and tied it up. Bill clambered from the boat and barked farewell to the ladies. He had enjoyed his boat ride but was happy to be on dry land again.

"Come and see us again sometime, you old sea dog!" the ladies yelled, waving him goodbye.

SOMETHING FISHY

Bill hadn't got far down the quayside when he noticed a pile of neglected fish, jellyfish and squid lying on the flagstones. It smelt like the pile had been there for quite some time, slowly rotting in the mid-day sun. He went over and gave it a good sniff. Never in all his life had he smelt such a rich, ripe smell. It was without doubt the King of all Disgusting Odours.

Bill hesitated. Even he wasn't sure what he was about to do – perhaps this smell was too much, even for him. Perhaps, on this occasion he should say no and simply walk

away. But then he thought that this was a once in a lifetime opportunity. He had to be brave and go for it. He flipped himself over onto the squidgy sea-creatures and wriggled around, letting the rancid stink soak into his fur, which was still sticky from the candyfloss.

By rolling around in the slimy fish, Bill made the stink ten times worse. It was so bad that some fishermen nearby, people well used to the pong of rotting stuff, were forced to cover their faces.

"Get away from there you dirty beast!" one of them squawked, and he threw his tin teacup at Bill.

Bill jumped to his feet, extremely proud of his new perfume, and quickly trotted out of the harbour.

Now it was time to find his family.

Bill didn't have the foggiest idea which way to go to find them. He wandered this way, then that way. He trotted down the unfamiliar streets and alleyways of the seaside town hoping to find the beach. Because he was a dog he couldn't ask anyone for help;and anyway, he stank so badly that no one would come anywhere near him.

He sat down by the roadside, and just when he started to think that he would have to spend the rest of his life as a wild, homeless dog, living on scraps and bones pulled from the bins (an idea he quite liked), a car suddenly squealed to a halt right next to him. The doors flew open and out jumped Bill's family. They looked shocked, then surprised, then delighted.

"It's you! It really is you!" cried Jasmine.

"We thought we'd lost you," said Angus. "We've been driving around for ages trying to find you."

"You were supposed to stay in the car," said Dad.

Then his nose twitched.

"Hell's bells! What is that atrocious smell?" He looked down at Bill. "It can't be... not even Bill... could smell... that bad." Dad's voice trailed away as he looked down at Bill, who was proudly grinning up at him.

"Yes," said Mum, "it's Bill."

The family folded the roof down on the car and got Bill on board.

Mum handed out handkerchiefs for everyone to wear over their faces to keep the worst of the stink out, and away they drove; looking like a family of bank robbers off to do a job.

Even with the roof down driving at top speed (and with the handkerchiefs on), the smell was almost unbearable.

"Must – get – home," Dad croaked, nearly gagging on his words.

They were just leaving Frosbie-on-Sea when Dad saw a sign at the side of the road.

It said: CAR WASH.

"That's it!" he cried, and pulled in.

He drove up to the entrance of the car wash, straightened his legs so he could get some money out of his pocket, and plonked the coins in the machine.

"What are you doing?" asked Mum.

"We're going for a wash," answered Dad.

"But – the roof isn't on," said Mum.

"I know," said Dad. He pulled the handkerchief down from his face and gave Mum a broad grin.

The next moment the car was pulled into the mouth of the carwash. There was no turning back now. Two vertical columns either side of the car suddenly sprang into

life. Whirling madly, their frothy clothy tassels whipped at the car.

"AAAAARGH!" everyone yelled.

A third column, this one horizontal, descended from the roof. It span and thrashed relentlessly, moving ever closer to the cowering family. Then it was upon them like a crazy hurricane, while soapy jets of water sprayed at them, soaking them through and through.

Then came the steam. It hissed through the family's hair (and most importantly, Bill's fur) and billowed through their clothes like a scorching tropical wind.

"OOOAAAAWW!" everyone screamed.

At last the car came out the other end. Everyone had shocked expressions on their faces – it had been the strangest and most frightening thing they had ever experienced together as a family.

"That was a stupid thing to do," said Mum, whose hair had frizzed up like a bush.

But Dad, however, had no regrets. "No more Smelly Bill," he said triumphantly, turning to look at their beloved, and extremely fluffy, pet. And it was true. Bill no longer stank.

"Now open the doors everyone," said Dad, "and let all this soapy water out."

Epilogue

Home Is Where the Fart Is

It was early evening by the time the family arrived home. They traipsed into the house exhausted from their weekend adventure.

Mum made hot chocolate for everyone and they all collapsed onto the sofa to watch a bit of telly before bed.

A reporter on the local news appeared on the screen, standing in a familiar field.

"And this is the campsite where the monster was seen!" explained the reporter. "Mr Frank Plumpton-Smythe was the

first person to see the beast." The reporter turned to speak to a man with a large bushy moustache.

"Oh look!" said Jasmine, "that's the man who camped next to us."

"It was horrible!" shouted the man. "I've seen some horrible creatures in my life, I've eaten a few too. But this thing was like nothing on Earth!"

Then on the screen there appeared an artist's impression of what the monster looked like.

"Hmmm," said Dad suspiciously, "it looks a bit like Bill if you ask me."

"More news!" said the newsman in the studio. "Woman trapped at Kennels. Miss Grinder of Sunny Meadow Kennels spent the weekend locked in one of her cages.

Too traumatised to give a full interview, she could say only one word – 'BILL'.

"Oh dear," said Dad, hardly able to look.

"And now on a lighter note," continued the newsman, breaking into a smile. "Frosbie-on-Sea was the location for one of the most remarkable sights of the summer - a candyfloss dog riding a large inflatable Banana!"

"Isn't that Bill?" said Mum

"Bill?" Dad shouted, getting up from the sofa. "What have you been up to, you naughty dog? Bill? BILL?"

But Bill couldn't hear him. He was on his back, in his basket, in the kitchen, fast asleep, dreaming of chasing bright yellow candyfloss rabbits ... and blowing off.

It had been a very busy weekend.

First published in 2010
by Meadowside Children's Books,
185 Fleet Street, London, EC4A 2HS
www.meadowsidebooks.com

A CIP catalogue record for this book
is available from the British Library
1 2 3 4 5 6 7 8 9 10

Printed in China